To Jaden,
With love from Grandma & Grandpa
June 2008

Chuf S Bau

ISBN 1-893622-17-7

Library of Congress Catalog Card Number: 2005935408

10 9 8 7 6 5 4 3 2 1

Printed in the United States of America

Dedication

We dedicate this book to a dear friend–our Washington, D.C., "mom"–Ambassador Esther Coopersmith, a supporter of music and the arts in our community and a leader in improving relations among nations and in promoting goodwill and dialogue in our capital and in capitals everywhere. Thank you for your friendship, support and inspiration and for your service to our country and the people of the world. Bravo for our Diva of Diplomacy!

— **P.W.B and C.S.B.**

Acknowledgements

We wish to acknowledge the help and support of the terrific team at The Kennedy Center and the National Symphony Orchestra in the creation of this book, including Ann Stock, the Center's Vice President of Institutional Affairs; Neil Schwartz, the Center's Director of Retail Operations, Patricia O'Kelly, the NSO's Managing Director of Media Relations; Jennifer Leed, Special Projects Manager for the NSO; Rita Shapiro, Executive Director of the NSO, and of course, the NSO's very own Maestro, Leonard Slatkin, Music Director. We also thank Stephen A. Schwarzman, Chairman of the Center, and Michael M. Kaiser, the Center's President, for their support of this project.

— **P.W.B and C.S.B.**

Little Wolfgang helps the Maestro Mouse find his missing baton.
Now find Wolfgang hidden in every illustration in the book!

The audience grows silent and the concert hall grows dim—
The stage is set, the lights go up and someone says, "It's him!"
The master of Rachmaninoff, of Beethoven and Strauss—
A truly great conductor—now presenting Maestro Mouse!

The Maestro is incomparable, the critics all agree.
He leads the National Symphony Orchestra in Washington, D.C.,
At the John F. Kennedy Center for the Performing Arts,
Named for a special president who touched our thoughts and hearts.

The orchestra's musicians are the finest in the land.
They wait for Maestro patiently, await his guiding hand,
Await not just instruction, but the Maestro's inspiration!
Quiet, now—the Maestro is so deep in concentration…

He steps on the conductor's box and turns to take a bow,
Then turns back to the orchestra, a furrow in his brow.
Then suddenly, he stops and stares—it looks like something's wrong!
He turns and shouts, "My goodness gracious! My baton is gone!"

The crowd cries out, "Oh, no! Impossible! How can it be?
With no baton, there is no tune, no notes—no symphony!"
The hall is in a panic now—the orchestra, a flurry,
When suddenly some children rush the stage—come on now, hurry!

"Maestro Mouse," the children said, "We're here to help, you'll see!
Your baton—we'll find it fast! We'll solve this mystery!
We'll search throughout the orchestra, we'll search in every nook!
We'll search in every instrument, each cranny and each crook!"

They started in the section where the orchestra begins
In many compositions, very softly—violins!
But they didn't find it in the strings or any of the cases—
A look of disappointment came across their furry faces.

The grand piano stood nearby—they raced to look inside
To see if somewhere in it a baton might try to hide!
But no, it wasn't in the bench or in-between the keys,
It wasn't in the pedals, either, or in the melodies!

Xylophone

Harp

Cymbals

It wasn't in the xylophone, the cymbals or the harp
(Though someone accidentally plucked a beautiful F-sharp).
They looked inside the French horns, too, to see what they could see—
It wasn't there—and neither was it in the timpani!

They searched the trumpets and trombones, but once again, alas,
They only thing they find in them was lots of twisted brass.
They looked inside the woodwinds next—the flutes and piccolo,
The clarinets, the big bassoon and oboes—oh, but no!

Tuba

They looked inside the tuba, too, so big and round and stout.
They turned it upside down, but no baton came tumbling out.
They ran to check the other strings, the cellos and the basses,
The violas, too, and then outside to look in other places.

They looked around the Hall of States
and the bust of JFK,
But they came back empty-handed,
to the orchestra's dismay.
The Maestro kept up hope in the
crescendo of the hunt,
As did the anxious patrons,
in their seats from back to front.

But shortly, quickly, it was clear, as everyone had feared,
The baton the Maestro loved so much had simply disappeared!
"Come here," the grateful Maestro said, "Come all you children, now,
I thank you for your help, young friends, and please, please, take a bow."

And as they walked across the stage to follow his command,
A little mouse named Wolfgang turned and shook the Maestro's hand.
Then Wolfgang noticed something he could simply not believe:
He saw the lost baton—stuck right inside the Maestro's sleeve!

Wolfgang shouted, "Maestro, look! I have found your lost baton!
It's right there, tucked inside your sleeve! Now the concert can go on!"
The embarrassed Maestro mumbled, "My dear friends, I must confess:
I forgot I slipped it in there in my absentmindedness!"

"Please forgive me," he continued. And they did, of course, because
He's their one and only Maestro. They responded with applause!
"Thank you, friends," the Maestro said. "Now be quiet, if you please—
We'll begin our program shortly with Beethoven's *Ode to Cheese*."

He turned and tapped the music stand—the orchestra was ready.
He held up his baton above, so confident and steady.
Then suddenly, he pulled it down, across and in a flash--
The trumpets started pealing and the cymbals clanged and crashed!

The orchestra was wonderful—it played so brilliantly
On that warm September night in Washington, D.C.,
Thanks to a great conductor, the amazing Maestro Mouse,
Who had again—with genius, skill and grace—brought down the house!

Educational Notes for Parents and Teachers

The Symphony Orchestra

A symphony orchestra is a group of musicians who play particular, individual instruments together to make music. It is usually made up of four major sections: strings, woodwinds, brass and percussion. The **strings** section is the largest and includes violins, violas, cellos and double basses. The **woodwind** section includes flutes, clarinets, oboes and bassoons. The **brass** section includes French horns, trumpets, trombones and tubas. The **percussion** section is comprised of a variety of instruments that produce sound by being struck, scraped, shaken or plucked. This section typically includes the timpani (kettle drums), bass drum, cymbals, triangle, harp, piano and sometimes a xylophone, depending on the composition. In a modern symphony orchestra, there can be from a few dozen musicians to more than 100. The **conductor,** often called "maestro," is the leader of the orchestra. The maestro determines the seating of the musicians in the orchestra and directs them in making music together.

To learn more about a symphony orchestra and its instruments, visit the National Symphony Orchestra's "Meet the Musicians" homepage at www.nationalsymphony.org/meetthemusicians.

The National Symphony Orchestra

The National Symphony Orchestra, founded in 1931, has been committed to artistic excellence and music education throughout its history. In 1986, the National Symphony became the artistic affiliate of The John F. Kennedy Center for the Performing Arts, the nation's center for the performing arts, where it has presented a concert season annually since the Center opened in 1971. The Orchestra itself numbers 100 musicians, presenting a 52-week season of approximately 175 concerts each year. These include a classical subscription series, pops series and one of the country's most extensive educational programs.

Celebrating its 75th season in 2005-2006, the National Symphony regularly participates in events of national and international importance, including performances for state occasions, presidential inaugurations and official holiday celebrations. Through its tours of four continents and performances for heads of state, the National Symphony also fills an important international role.

The National Symphony has a strong commitment to the development of America's artistic resources. Through the John and June Hechinger Commissioning Fund for New Orchestral Works, the Orchestra has commissioned more than 50 works, including cycles of fanfares and encores. These commissions are representative of the diverse influences in American composition today. The National Symphony has also long been distinguished for its nurturing of emerging American conductors; that commitment has escalated with the creation of the National Conducting Institute in 2000 by Music Director Leonard Slatkin.

Another important project is the National Symphony Orchestra American Residencies for The Kennedy Center. This venture encompasses sharing all elements of classical symphonic music with a specific region of the United States, exploring the diversity of musical influences and giving the region a musical voice in the nation's center for the performing arts through exchanges, training programs, and commissions. Established in 1992, the project has taken the NSO to 14 states through 2005.

For more information on the National Symphony Orchestra, visit www.nationalsymphony.org.

The John F. Kennedy Center for the Performing Arts

The John F. Kennedy Center for the Performing Arts, overlooking the Potomac River in Washington, D.C., is America's living memorial to President Kennedy, our 35th President. As the nation's busiest performing arts facility, it houses seven theaters and stages and welcomes two million audience members each year. Center-related touring productions, television and radio broadcasts welcome 20 million more.

The Center presents the greatest examples of music, dance and theater; supports artists in the creation of new work and serves the nation as a leader in arts education. With its artistic affiliate, the National Symphony Orchestra, the Center's achievements as a commissioner, producer and nurturer of developing artists have resulted in over 300 theatrical productions, dozens of new ballets, operas and musical works. The Center has produced and co-produced *Annie*; the American premiere of *Les Misérables*; the highly acclaimed *Sondheim Celebration*; the three-play *Tennessee Williams Explored,* as well as the multi-disciplined *A New America: The 1940s and the Arts.* The Center's Emmy and Peabody Award-winning *The Kennedy Center Honors* is broadcast annually on the CBS Television Network; *The Kennedy Center Mark Twain Prize* is seen on PBS.

Each year, more than 11 million people nationwide take part in innovative and effective education programs initiated by the Center—performances, lecture/demonstrations, open rehearsals, dance and music residencies, master classes, competitions for young actors and musicians and workshops for teachers. These programs have become models for communities across the country.

As part of The Kennedy Center's "Performing Arts for Everyone" outreach program, the Center and the National Symphony Orchestra stage more than 400 free performances of music, dance and theater by artists from throughout the world each year on the Center's main stages and every evening on the Millennium Stage. The Center also offers the nation's largest Specially Priced Tickets program for students, seniors, persons with disabilities, military personnel and others with fixed low incomes.

To learn more about The Kennedy Center, visit www.kennedy-center.org.